W9-BTM-373

THE BIRTHDAY WISH

By Richard Matsuura, PhD.
Ruth Matsuura, M.D.

Diena Arruda

Minda Barcelona

Rodney Cabison

Denise Carreira

Troy Carriaga

Douglas Delmar

Ian Enitan

William Gonsalves

Mark Gouveia

Earl Hasegawa

Wade Herlicska

Shawn Kahalewai

Keenan Kahalioumi

Jordan Kahele

Malania Kapika

Reed Kepaa

Patrick Leslie

Edwin Nabarro

Alvina Naone

Keldon Ogawa

Hans Santiago

Lynette Santiago

Barbara Spencer

Melissa Waugh

Roxanne Wong

Mrs. Karen Tengan

Mrs. Ellen Takazawa

Illustrated by Linus Chao

TO THE CHILDREN OF HAWAII
AND MISS FANNY HOWE

Library of Congress Catalog
Card Number 95-72693

THE BIRTHDAY WISH

In the coastal range of the Waianae mountains lived a Hawaiian family of six children.

Nona, the youngest, was five years old on this day. Her mother told her that there would be no birthday party because there was no extra money. Nona ran out of the house crying. As she sat on the sandy beach sobbing, Grandfather came and sat beside her to comfort her.

"When I was your age," he said, "I made many birthday cakes with the sand and put a candle on each of them. Then I would make a birthday wish."

"What's a birthday wish?" sniffed Nona wiping the tears from her cheek.

Grandfather was surprised, "You mean you never heard about the birthday wish?" Nona slowly shook her head. So Grandfather settled down and began this story . . .

Long ago there was a poor orphan girl who lived on a dairy farm. She was very bright and hard working. From sunrise to sunset she did her chores on the farm happily. But of all the work she did, she loved most to deliver the milk and eggs to the townspeople. Everyone looked forward to seeing the girl because she was so cheerful and generous, and always had a helpful wish for everyone.

One day, as she stopped by the dressmaker's shop to deliver the milk, she saw her having a difficult time sewing with a hooked pin and thread. "I wish you had a needle with an eye," said the orphan girl.

"Why, that is a stupendous idea," said the seamstress. "You have just given me a tool to make my work easier and enjoyable!"

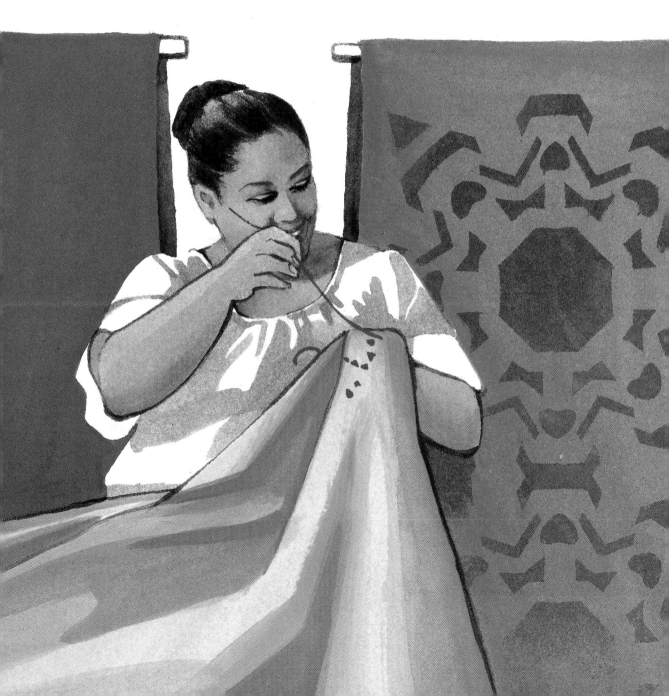

The girl then delivered the eggs to the bakery and saw the baker sad and worried. "What is the matter?" she asked.

The baker replied, "The King wants a special birthday cake for his one year old son, and I only know how to make a simple birthday cake."

"If I were the Prince," she replied, "I would wish for a candle on top of my birthday cake to make it glow."

The baker leaped with joy! "Oh, thank you," said the excited baker, "you have just given me an idea for the special cake!"

As the orphan girl walked down the street, she stopped to watch a carpenter building a house. The carpenter was having a difficult time. He was balancing himself on a pile of boxes so he could nail the boards high above his head. As he came tumbling down to the ground, the orphan girl went to help him and wished that he had a stairway made of two long poles and cross pieces so he could climb to the high places without falling. The aching carpenter began to smile. "Thank you! You have just given me an idea for a ladder."

The young girl sang as she went to deliver the eggs and milk to an old couple living by the stream. On her way she saw the laundryman, angrily chasing the cows and dogs away from the clean clothes he had laid on the grass to dry. The animals had soiled all the clothes! "Don't be angry," called the orphan girl. "What I wish you had is a long rope tied to the trees to hang your wash."

The laundryman scratched his head, and then smiled and replied, "How can I remain angry when you have just given me an idea for a clothesline." The laundryman waved and thanked her.

On the way home, she met an old man with a wooden leg hobbling down the street. "May I give you a ride on the milk wagon?" she asked.

"No thank you," said the man, "I have but a short distance to walk."

"I wish you had a stick that you could lean on when you walk," said the orphan girl.

"Why, that's a brilliant idea," he beamed. "I will make myself a wooden crutch. Thank you for your offer of a ride and your helpful wish! Now, you'd better hurry home. I see a storm is coming."

The orphan girl rode toward home but the thunderstorm started before she reached the farm. She was wet and cold when she drove into the barn. Unhitching the milk wagon, she dried the horse and went to her room. As she lay shivering in her bed, she looked out of her tiny window and wished for one wish. Her simple prayer was heard.

An angel appeared before the orphan girl and said, "You may have one wish." The girl thought about how she wished to be the richest girl on earth, or the most beautiful Queen, but then a smile came on her face.

"What is your wish?" asked the angel.

The orphan girl hesitated for a moment and said, "I wish that every child will have a wish on his birthday."

"So shall it be," said the angel.

That was the beginning of the birthday wish and that is why every child to this day has a birthday wish.

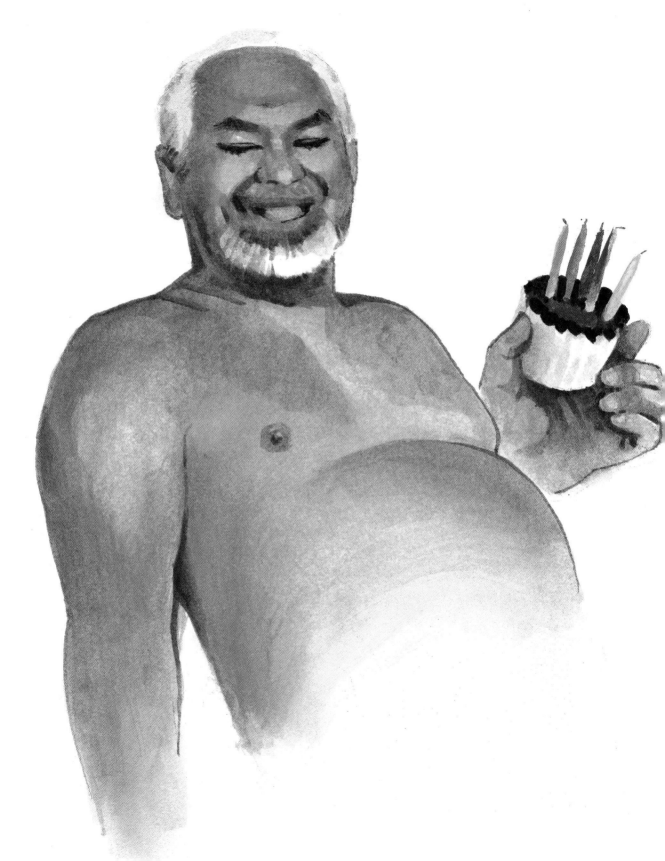

Grandfather got up, stretched, and then sat down again next to Nona. He took a small cup cake from a bag he had been carrying and placed five little candles on it. He lit the candles and asked her to make a wish and blow out the candles. She looked at him happily, surprised by his gift. She closed her eyes for a few minutes and then with one breath blew out all the candles. Nona gave half of the little cup cake to Grandfather and hugged him tightly. She whispered, "I wished every child could be as happy as I am." Grandfather smiled and said, "Birthday wishes will come true."

THE END